With love to Steve, Jamie, and Fay—
so happy you're part of our troop! —A.W.P.

To Mom, Dad, Andy, and Amy —J.F.

Farrar Straus Giroux Books for Young Readers
An imprint of Macmillan Publishing Group, LLC
120 Broadway, New York, NY 10271
mackids.com

Our books may be purchased in bulk for promotional, educational, or business use. Please contact your local bookseller
or the Macmillan Corporate and Premium Sales Department at (800) 221-7945 ext. 5442 or
by email at MacmillanSpecialMarkets@macmillan.com.

Library of Congress Cataloging-in-Publication Data
Names: Paul, Ann Whitford, author. | Fleck, Jay, illustrator.
Title: Who loves Little Lemur? / Ann Whitford Paul ; pictures by Jay Fleck.
Description: First edition. | New York: Farrar Straus Giroux, 2021. | Includes facts about lemurs. | Audience: Ages 3–6. | Audience:
Grades K–1. | Summary: A little lemur goes through the day surrounded by family who love and help him.
Identifiers: LCCN 2020023288 | ISBN 9780374388478 (hardcover)
Subjects: CYAC: Stories in rhyme. | Lemurs—Fiction. | Family life—Fiction. | Love—Fiction.
Classification: LCC PZ8.3.P273645 Wh 2021 | DDC [E]—dc23
LC record available at https://lccn.loc.gov/2020023288.

First edition, 2021
Book design by Aram Kim and Melisa Vuong
Color separations by Bright Arts (H.K.) Ltd.
Printed in China by Hung Hing Off-set Printing Co. Ltd., Heshan City, Guangdong Province

ISBN 978-0-374-38847-8 (hardcover)
1 3 5 7 9 10 8 6 4 2

Who Loves Little Lemur?

Ann Whitford Paul

Pictures by Jay Fleck

Farrar Straus Giroux
New York

Who loves Little Lemur?

On a giant island in a faraway sea,
Mama snuggles Little Lemur
near the tamarind tree.

When the mist creeps away,
and the sun climbs up,
she nuzzles and nurses her precious pup.

Papa stretches, gambols about,

and tweaks Little Lemur's short black snout.

Grandma plucks Little Lemur's bugs
and squeezes him tight in furry hugs.

Grandpa joins them. Together they sit,
facing the sun, warming a bit.

Who loves Little Lemur?

Sister tugs his long ringed tail.

Brother runs quick, rubs Little Lemur's hurt,

then tussle! *Tum-tumble* in the dirt!

Auntie beckons Little Lemur
to *prancity-prance.*

The whole troop joins in
their *jump-jump* dance.

Little Lemur flops down. Uncle shares his lunch.

Yummy fig!

Munch! Munch! Munch!

**Who loves
Little Lemur?**

Cousins chase him up
a sheer cliff wall.

Screech!
Squeal!
Lemur squall!

What's wrong, Little Lemur?

Oh no!

Mama's coming.
Don't let go!

He rides on her back, down,

down,

down

to the soft and

safe grassy ground.

Dribble! Dribble!
Pitter, patter.
Rain falls.
Splitter, splatter.

Huddle under the ledge of rock.

Thunder! Lightning!

Dribble, drop-drop.

The troop hovers close, keeps Little Lemur dry.

The rain stops.

Clouds leave the sky.

Night darkens to star-speckled black.

Papa feeds him his cricket snack.

Who loves Little Lemur?

So many do —

Mama, Papa,

grandparents,

Sister, Brother,

Auntie, Uncle,

cousins,

the whole busy troop.

And Little Lemur trills, "Aah ooh, aah ooh," lemur speak for *I love you, too.*

Facts about Lemurs

* Little Lemur lives off the coast of Africa on Madagascar, the fourth largest island in the world.

* There are more than one hundred different species of lemurs. Little Lemur belongs to the ring-tailed lemur group.

* Lemur young are called pups.

* Lemurs are social and live in groups, called troops, of up to about thirty. They are made up of several female lemurs, their offspring, and the males, who mostly huddle nearby.

* Lemurs are great climbers and leapers, but their tails, unlike monkeys', cannot grasp.

* Lemurs eat leaves, fruit, bark, sap, and bugs.